Murphy and Kate

Murphy and Kate

by Ellen Howard

illustrated by Mark Graham

SIMON & SCHUSTER BOOKS FOR YOUNG READERS

SIMON & SCHUSTER BOOKS FOR YOUNG READERS
An imprint of Simon & Schuster Children's Publishing Division
1230 Avenue of the Americas, New York, New York 10020
Text copyright © 1995 by Ellen Howard
Illustrations copyright © 1995 by Mark Graham
SIMON & SCHUSTER BOOKS FOR YOUNG READERS
is a trademark of Simon & Schuster.
Designed by David Neuhaus.
The text for this book is set in 15.5 point Garamond #3.
The illustrations were done in oils.
Manufactured in the United States of America
10 9 8 7 6 5 4 3 2 1
Library of Congress Cataloging-in-Publication Data
Howard, Ellen. Murphy and Kate/by Ellen Howard:
illustrated by Mark Graham. Summary: Kate and her dog Murphy
are best friends, and when Murphy dies Kate does not think she
can ever be happy again. [1. Dogs—Fiction. 2. Death—Fiction.]
I. Graham, Mark, 1952- ill. II. Title PZ7.H83274Mu 1994
[E]—dc20   CIP AC 93-26002
ISBN 0-671-79775-1

For Kathryn and Murphy,
and for Annabeth
in memory of Lilli
—E.H.

To Mom
—M.G.

Kate was fourteen when Murphy died. Murphy was the same age as Kate.

That was *old* for a dog, everyone said. Murphy was tired, everyone said. He had lived a good, long life.

But Kate wasn't old, and she wasn't tired. She still had a good, long life to live. Without Murphy.

She didn't know how she could do it.

You will feel happy again, everyone said. After a while, you'll forget.

Kate couldn't imagine feeling happy again. Not without Murphy.

Murphy had come to live with Kate's family when Kate was just a baby. Mom and Dad had thought he'd be a good playmate for Kate's big sisters.

But Murphy knew better than that.

The big sisters had each other to play with. It was Baby Kate who needed a friend.

Right away Kate loved the tickle of Murphy's whiskers and the warm wetness of his tongue. She loved the plumpness of his middle that went "yip" when she squeezed. She loved the happy thumping of his tail.

They would play pounce-on-baby's-blanket and chase-doggie's-tail and who-can-crawl-farthest-before-Mom-brings-us-back.

When Kate had breakfast in her high chair, Murphy had his on the floor.

When Kate chewed on Mom's purse strap, Murphy chewed on Dad's shoe.

They took their naps together.

For a while, Kate grew bigger and Murphy grew bigger, too. But when Murphy was as big as he was going to get, Kate kept right on growing.

She grew big enough to walk by herself. (Murphy had always known how.) She grew big enough to talk in words. (Murphy never learned.) She grew big enough to play with friends, but her *best* friend was Murphy.

They played dress-up with Kate's doll clothes. (Murphy liked rides in the buggy.)

They went visiting up and down the street. Kate taught
Murphy to walk standing up.

"One step at a time," she would say to him, holding his paw
in her hand.

And, one step at a time, Murphy learned to walk on his hind
legs, paw in hand with Kate.

When Kate grew big enough to go to school, Murphy would watch from the window as she and her sisters waited on the corner. Then, after the school bus had taken Kate away, Murphy would lie down with his chin on his paws and sigh a lonely sigh. He took his nap by himself. He followed Mom around the house, dropping his ball at her feet.

"Not now, Murphy," Mom would say. "I don't have time to play."

But after school Kate had time for Murphy. They played ball. (Murphy was good at fetching.) They played swinging. When Kate swung, Murphy barked. Then Kate helped Murphy to sit on the swing. (Though, usually, he slipped off.) They went walking paw in hand.

Kate kept right on growing. She grew big enough to ride a
bike. (Murphy ran alongside, his tongue hanging out.) She
grew big enough to have a friend stay overnight. (Murphy slept
between them.) Sometimes Kate didn't come straight home
from school; but whenever she came, Murphy was waiting.

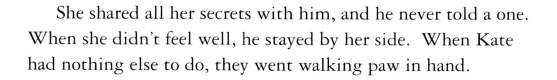

She shared all her secrets with him, and he never told a one.
When she didn't feel well, he stayed by her side. When Kate
had nothing else to do, they went walking paw in hand.

And Kate kept right on growing. She grew so big, she began to fuss with her hair. (Murphy would wait for her outside the bathroom door.) She grew so big, she had to do lots of homework. (Murphy would sit under her desk.) She grew so big, some of her friends were boys. But when she remembered, Kate's *best* friend was Murphy.

As Kate grew bigger, she didn't have as much time to play, but Murphy didn't seem to mind. He took long, long naps under the old tree swing. He sat at her feet during dinner. (Sometimes she slipped him tidbits.) He lay beside her when she talked on the phone. (She scratched his ears as she talked.) Whenever Kate came home, Murphy was waiting.

The day Murphy wasn't waiting, Kate didn't notice at first. ("I didn't even notice!" she cried later.)

As she came through the door, the phone was ringing, and she talked for a long time with her friend. She had lots of homework. Her favorite show was on that night.

It was almost bedtime before Kate wondered, Where's Murphy?

She found him in his napping place beneath the old tree swing.

"Murphy," she called.

But Murphy didn't come. He lifted his head. He thumped his tail once. Then his head fell back on his paws.

Kate ran to kneel beside him. "Murphy, Murphy?" she said.

Murphy sighed and looked at Kate. Then something bright went from his eyes.

She hugged him hard. She called his name. But Murphy was dead.

Mom found a box to put Murphy in. Dad dug a grave by the tree. Kate wrapped him in his blanket, for already he grew cold.

A hard, hurting lump was in Kate's throat. Tears wet her cheeks, and there was no Murphy to lick them away. No whiskers to tickle. No thumping tail. No small paw in her hand.

By the time Murphy had been buried, it was late.

"Past time for bed," Mom said.

"How *can* I sleep?" said Kate.

Even in the dark, Kate could feel the emptiness of Murphy's basket. But her bed was warm, and her eyelids were heavy.

Kate slept.

In the morning Kate saw that Murphy's bowl had been taken away.

"How can I eat breakfast?" said Kate.

But her toast was golden with butter, and her juice was foamy and cold.

Kate ate.

No Murphy watched as she walked to the corner.

"How *can* I go to school?" said Kate.

But the school bus came as it always did, and Kate went to school.

The choir was practicing for the spring concert.

"How *can* I sing?" said Kate.

The lump in her throat stopped the song. When the music was soft, tears came to her eyes. But all around her voices were lifting, and Kate sang.

"How *can* I ever feel happy again?" said Kate.

It was like Murphy, learning to walk on hind legs.

"One step at a time," said Kate.

You'll feel happy again, everyone had said.

And one day at a time, one night at a time, one word, one song, one smile at a time, Kate did feel happy again.

But everyone also had said, you'll forget.

And Kate knew better than that.

It wasn't forgetting Murphy that made her feel happy. It was remembering him.